KIDS' SPORTS STORIES

BASEBALL BATTLE

by Elliott Smith

illustrated by Alex Patrick

PICTURE WINDOW BOOKS
a capstone imprint

Kids' Sports Stories is published by Picture Window Books,
an imprint of Capstone.
1710 Roe Crest Drive, North Mankato, Minnesota 56003
www.capstonepub.com

Library of Congress Cataloging-in-Publication Data
Names: Smith, Elliott, 1976- author. | Patrick, Alex, illustrator.
Title: Baseball battle / by Elliott Smith ; illustrated by Alex Patrick.
Description: North Mankato, Minnesota : Picture Window Books,
an imprint of Capstone, [2021] | Series: Kids' sports stories | Audience:
Ages 5-7. | Audience: Grades K-1. | Summary: Lifelong friends
Jackson and Logan are moving up from T-ball to baseball,
but when both boys want to play first base they must decide
if baseball is more important than their friendship.
Identifiers: LCCN 2020035179 (print) | LCCN 2020035180 (ebook) | ISBN
9781515882435 (hardcover) | ISBN 9781515883524 (paperback) | ISBN
9781515891765 (pdf) | ISBN 9781515892762 (kindle edition)
Subjects: CYAC: Baseball—Fiction. | Friendship—Fiction.
Classification: LCC PZ7.1.S626 Bap 2021 (print) | LCC PZ7.1.S626
(ebook) | DDC [E]—dc23
LC record available at https://lccn.loc.gov/2020035179
LC ebook record available at https://lccn.loc.gov/2020035180

Designer: Kyle Grenz

Printed in the United States   4430

TABLE OF CONTENTS

Glossary

 **error**—a mistake made while fielding

 **fielding**—the act of catching or stopping a baseball

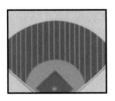 **outfield**—the part of a baseball field past the bases

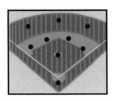 **position**—the spot where a player stands when his or her team is in the field

Chapter 1
A NEW SPORT

"Throw it!" Jackson shouted to his friend Logan.

The boys were playing catch in Jackson's backyard. They pretended a runner was racing to home plate. Logan scooped up the baseball. He threw it hard, right into Jackson's glove. *SMACK!*

"Out!" Logan shouted. "Got him!"

The boys gave each other a high-five and took a water break.

"I can't wait for baseball to start," Jackson said. "It's going to be fun."

Last year, the friends had played T-ball. They had hit the ball off a small stand. This year, their coach would pitch the ball to them.

"I hope I can hit," Logan said. "Coach might throw pretty hard."

"You'll do great!" Jackson said. "We can practice hitting tomorrow. Just don't break any windows!"

Jackson tossed the ball into the air. Logan jumped to grab it.

"I'm going to try out for first base," Logan said. "That's my favorite **position**. The ball always comes to you."

Jackson frowned. *He* wanted to play first base. What if Coach picked Logan instead of him? Logan was really good at sports. Plus, he was bigger. Jackson's stomach started to hurt.

"Hey, look alive, buddy!" Logan said.
He flipped the ball to Jackson.

Jackson shook off his bad feelings.
"Got it," he said, catching the ball easily.
"Let's keep throwing. We have to be ready
for our first practice!"

Chapter 2

NOT THE BEST

It was the first day of baseball practice. Jackson and Logan gathered with their teammates on the field. They tapped their gloves and smiled.

Coach blew her whistle. "OK, let's get started," she said. "Welcome to baseball! We're going to learn lots of new skills here. And we're going to have lots of fun doing it!"

Batting practice came first. Coach pitched. Logan tried, but he didn't get many hits.

Jackson hit nearly every ball. On his last swing, he hit the ball hard over Coach's head. "Nice swing, Jackson!" she said.

Jackson felt great. He couldn't wait for fielding practice. He would show Coach that he was the best choice for first base.

At fielding practice, Logan grabbed every ball thrown to him at first base. He stretched. He leaped. He caught some of the worst throws.

Jackson, on the other hand, made one
error after another. He missed throws.
He dropped balls. Everything went wrong.

At the end of practice, Coach told the players which positions they'd play. "Logan, you're on first base," she said.

"Cool. Thanks!" Logan said. He looked over at Jackson and smiled. Jackson didn't smile back.

"Jackson, keep practicing," Coach continued. "We may try you at first base later on. For now, you're in the **outfield**. And keep swinging that bat hard for us!"

When Coach was done, the team headed home. Jackson left without saying goodbye to Logan. He got into his mom's car and threw his glove onto the seat.

"What's wrong, Jackson?" his mom asked.

Jackson shook his head. "I don't think Logan and I are friends anymore," he said quietly.

Chapter 3
FRIENDSHIP FIRST

Jackson's mom turned around in her seat. "I'm sure that's not true," she said. "Why would you think that?"

"I wanted to play first base, and now Logan gets to!" Jackson said. "He always gets the good positions! He got quarterback in flag football. He got shooting guard in basketball. It's not fair."

Jackson's mom smiled. "Remember the school musical last fall? You and Logan both wanted the same part. When you got it, Logan was happy for you. That's being a good friend."

Jackson thought about what his mom
said. Logan had even helped him learn
his lines. She was right. Logan was a
good friend.

"But I wasn't a good friend today,"
Jackson said. "I didn't tell Logan I was
happy for him. I didn't say goodbye either."

Jackson's mom reached out and patted
his shoulder. "Well, you can tell him how
you feel tomorrow, OK?" she said.

"Thanks, Mom," Jackson said.

The next day at practice, Jackson ran over to Logan. The two boys tapped their gloves and smiled.

"Sorry about yesterday," Jackson said. "I really wanted to play first base too. But I know you'll be awesome there. Still friends?"

"Of course," Logan said. "Friendship first, right?"

"Let's practice at my house this weekend," Jackson said. "You can help me get better at **fielding**."

"And you can help me get better at batting!" Logan said. "Teamwork!"

Just then, Coach blew her whistle. The
team gathered around her. Their first game
was two weeks away. No one was more
excited than Jackson and Logan.

TEAM PENNANT

Jackson and Logan's baseball team is the Elephants. Cheer them on by making a pennant!

What You Need:
- a large piece of construction paper
- scissors
- crayons or markers
- add-ons, such as glitter, stickers, or pom-poms
- glue (optional)

What You Do:
- Cut a pennant shape (a tall triangle) from the paper.
- Write "Go Elephants!" or "Go Team!" in big letters on the pennant.
- Decorate the pennant by drawing a picture of an elephant or baseball. Or glue on some add-ons. Be creative!

Take another look at this illustration. How do you think Jackson felt when his coach told him he would be playing in the outfield instead of first base?

Now pretend you are Jackson. Write a note to Logan congratulating him on getting to play first base.

ABOUT THE AUTHOR

Elliott Smith is a former sports reporter who covered athletes in all sports from high school to the pros. He is one of the authors of the Natural Thrills series about extreme outdoor sports. In his spare time, he likes playing sports with his two children, going to the movies, and adding to his collection of Pittsburgh Steelers memorabilia.

ABOUT THE ILLUSTRATOR

Alex Patrick was born in the Kentish town of Dartford in the southeast of England. He has been drawing for as long as he can remember. His life-long love for cartoons, picture books, and comics has shaped him into the passionate children's illustrator he is today. Alex loves creating original characters. He brings an element of fun and humor to each of his illustrations and is often found laughing to himself as he draws.